This book belongs to

Dedicated to Mum

Published by Lee Lamb from Lee Lamb Publishing Wanaka, New Zealand

ISBN 978-0-473-35991-1

First impression 2016 printed by Alliance Printers Ltd

Special thanks to

Penni Loffhagen from Tawhai Suffolk Stud and Mel Cleland for supplying photos.

There’s a lot of commotion down on the farm –
and it is almost time to go!
Everyone is getting their entries prepared
as it’s time for the A and P Show!

Mum gathers up her knitting and delicious baking,
while the kids juggle their entries with care.
The farmer tucks his prize winning pumpkin under his arm –
maybe this could be his year!

SHOW
MYW46N

The best six animals have been chosen to go,
because they stood out from the rest.
But being great on your own farm is one thing,
winning against others is the true test!

They have been well-trained during the year,
but there is still a lot of work to be done today.
The animals need to be sparkly and clean
so they look their best while out on display!

Tom practices his skills on the chickens as everything is loaded into the truck.

He is entered in the show dog trails - and he could win… with a bit of luck!

Jack has been chosen by the kids to represent the pets in the parade.

He is very proud to walk around the ring and wear the costumes they have made.

There are so many amazing sights and smells
as they arrive at the busy show grounds.
Candy floss, hot chips and dropped ice cream (yum!)
Sideshows, a Ferris wheel and merry-go-rounds!!

The dogs wish they could join the kids
as they race off to have some fun.
Oh what they would give for one dropped ice cream…
but they know there is work to be done.

SHOOT TO WIN
POULTRY
YTHING
$5 only
LUCKY DIP $2
FOOD
MENU
chips
hot dogs
PRODU
E • SHE

Tom is up first and is eager to get started,
but the sheep have another plan.
They make Tom work very hard to pen them
and he has to run as fast as he can!

Jack is up next and he is excited to get in the ring and beat the cat.

That was until he realises, it will be HIM wearing that hat…

The calf was doing much better, until the judge slipped on a cow pat –
instead of helping her get up he started EATING her flowery hat!

The little pony did her very best, even though she was small in size.

She trotted around the ring elegantly – and came out with second prize!!

The ram was full of confidence
as he strutted out to join the line.
The judges were impressed with his looks
and that his wool was so soft and fine.

The Jack Russell race is quite the event
with lots of small dogs giving one hundred percent.
Jack thinks it's rude when he gets to the race –
They have started without him, and set a fast pace!

He passes the terriers, overtaking them one by one.
Then he crosses the finish line ahead of everyone!
On the loud speaker, Jack hears his name
but the Jack Russell trophy is not his to claim.

Jack is a Huntaway, so he is not the right breed.
Understanding the rules is hard when you're a dog that can't read.
The farmer is grumpy and Jack doesn't know why,
so he decides next year he'll give it an even better try!

23

In the Produce Shed the veggies were impressive. There were some fine specimens in the group. Even though the farmer's pumpkin was a lot smaller, I'm sure it will still make yummy soup.

Mums knitting took out the top prize,
and her cake left the judges wanting more.
Her pikelets were winners in the kid's eyes,
but they had to do taste tests to be sure!

The children were thrilled to see they had done well too
and were eager to collect the prize money.
Some chose to save their winnings,
while others spent it on things that were useful, fast and funny.

Ghost Tra
BOUNCY CASTLE $2
DRIVE a DIGGER
JCB
ENTER IF YOU DAR
$2 LUCKY DI

Bag pipes sound out
at the end of the day
as the Highland Band
begins to play.

Draped in ribbons and awards,
they all strut their stuff.
But after one lap of the ring,
they have all had enough.

With the vehicles loaded up
it is now time to go,
Tomorrow will start the countdown
to next year's A and P Show.

SHOW